THE LAND OF
HUNGRY ARMADILLOS

Lawrence David   illustrated by Frédérique Bertrand

A Doubleday Book for Young Readers

A Doubleday Book for Young Readers
Published by
Random House Children's Books
a division of
Random House, Inc.
1540 Broadway
New York, New York 10036

Doubleday and the anchor with dolphin colophon are registered trademarks of
Random House, Inc.

Visit us on the Web! www.randomhouse.com/kids
Educators and librarians, for a variety of teaching tools, visit us at
www.randomhouse.com/teachers

Cataloging-in-Publication Data is available from the Library of Congress.
ISBN: 0-385-32698-X

The text of this book is set in 15-point Sassoon Sans Medium and Improv.
Book design by Trish P. Watts
Manufactured in the United States of America
May 2000
10 9 8 7 6 5 4 3 2 1

For Ajay Sahgal
—L.E.D.

For Emile and Pauline
—F.B.

"GIVE SOME CRAYONS TO YOUR SISTER,"
Gus's mother yelled from the kitchen.
"OR I'LL TAKE THEM ALL AWAY
AND NO ONE WILL DRAW."
Wendy reached for the box of crayons.
"Mom said to share."
Gus frowned as Wendy took the Rose Red, Boo-Hoo Blue,
and Slick Silver crayons.
He watched as she reached for a sheet of paper.
"Go get your own,"
he said, slamming his hand down on the pile.
Wendy stuck out her tongue and walked across the room. Gus
took a piece of paper and drew a land that had red mountains,
a lake of bubbling goo, and a line of hungry armadillos with
wide-open mouths.
In the center, he drew his little sister crying.
He looked at his drawing and grinned.

"WHAT IN THE WORLD . . . ?"
Gus and Wendy's mother said.
Gus looked up and saw his mother pointing at the wall,
where Wendy had scribbled a large, ugly crayon blotch.
"I drew a cupcake," she said.
"Why did you do that?" their mother asked.
"Gus wouldn't give me any paper," Wendy said.
"Gus!" their mother said. "Why can't you share?
You have plenty of paper."
"It's not my fault she's such a baby," Gus said.
"I'm not a baby!" Wendy screamed.
"Babies draw on walls," Gus told her.
"Babies can't share," Wendy said.
"That's enough," their mother interrupted.
"You can both go up to your rooms.
And don't come down until you've decided to behave."
Wendy cried and ran up to her room.
Gus began picking up the paper and crayons.
"And leave those here," his mother said.

Gus stared out of his bedroom window.
He had toys and games, but he didn't want to play with
them. He wanted to draw, but his sister had ruined that.
His mother came into the room.
"Are you ready to behave
and come down for dinner?" she asked.
"Your sister said she was sorry and cleaned up the wall."
"Well, I'm not sorry!" Gus told her.
"I'll never be a good brother to that baby."
His mother frowned.
"Then you'll just have to eat up here by yourself."
"I'm not hungry!" Gus growled.
His mother left the room without another word.

High up in the sky, a star winked. Gus shut his eyes and wished
for a box of crayons and a pad of paper all his own.
When he opened his eyes, a tall creature with pointy ears
and a long tail stood before him.
The creature smiled a sharp-toothed smile.
In his claws were the largest box
of crayons and the largest pad
of paper Gus had ever seen.

"Who are you?" Gus asked.

"I'm Zub," the creature said.

"You made a wish and here I am."

"Zub?" Gus asked. "All those crayons and all that paper are for me?" He held out his hands. Zub waved a finger. "They're all yours for a trade," he explained. "What will you give me in return?" Gus looked around his room. "How about a pair of purple socks or my Atomic Ace underwear?"

"I don't think so," Zub said.

"How about some old candy?"

"I don't think so," Zub said.

Gus laughed. "How about my little sister? Could you use her for anything?"

Zub smiled. "Oh, that would be a wonderful trade. I need help feeding my many hungry pets."

"Great!" Gus said happily.

He grabbed the paper and crayons Zub offered him and went to his desk.

He pulled the Grasshopper Green crayon from the box and drew a dragon's head.

"Have fun," Zub said. "Good night."

When Gus turned to say good-bye, Zub was already gone.

1.

Early the
next morning,

2.

Gus collected
his pictures.

WENDY!

6.

"Wendy?" he called out. No answer. He remembered how angry
he'd been with her the day before and the deal he'd made with
Zub. Oh, no, thought Gus. He searched the rest of the house.
He couldn't find Wendy anywhere.

ything?"

is desk.

gon's head.

3.

He rushed to his mother's
bedroom to show her what
he had drawn.

MOMMY

4.

She was still sleeping, so he went
to his sister's room.
The door was open.

WENDY

5.

There was no Wendy. On the wall above her bed,
Gus saw the picture he'd drawn of her favorite doll.
On top of the pile of pictures Gus held
was a new one he'd made for Wendy.

Gus returned to his room
and looked out at the sky.
The sun blazed, bright and golden.
No stars.
Gus shut his eyes and made a wish anyway.
"Zub, please bring Wendy home
and I'll give you all the paper
and crayons back," he said.
"I don't want them anymore.
I want my sister home.
I don't hate her.
I never meant for her really to be gone."

Suddenly Gus was no longer in his room.
Suddenly he was no longer home at all.
There was a flash of lightning and he
found himself in a strange land.

Everywhere he looked he saw people doing hard chores. One man rolled a
rock up a hill. As soon as he let go, the rock rolled back down. A large
armadillo nipped at his heels. The man moaned and pushed the rock up the
hill again. Nearby, a woman tried to fill a pool with water from a well.
Whenever she filled her bucket, the water all poured out
through holes in the bottom. An armadillo snapped at the woman's feet,
forcing her to do her chore over and over again.

As Gus searched for his sister and Zub,
he happened upon more armadillos.
A long line of the animals stretched far off into the distance.
Gus kept walking.
He finally spotted Wendy at the front of the line.
She was frantically mixing cupcake batter
and pouring it into molds.
She baked, iced, and then passed out cupcakes
to the waiting armadillos.
The hungry armadillos snatched the cupcakes
and swallowed them in one large gulp.
The minute an armadillo finished a cupcake,
it scuttled to the end of the line to wait for another.
"Wendy, what are you doing?" Gus asked.
Wendy scowled.
"I have to feed all the armadillos
because you traded me to Zub.
Why can't you ever be nice?"
Gus shook his head.
"I didn't think he would really
take you away,"
he explained.
"I'm sorry."

Then Zub appeared,
grinning a big grin.

Gus looked at him. "How long does Wendy have to do this?"
Zub laughed.
"Until the armadillos are no longer hungry.
But that will never happen.
My armadillos are always hungry.
All day and all night.
Just like everyone else in my land,
Wendy will have to do her job forever."
"But she's part of my family," Gus told him.
"My mother will miss her. I'll miss her."
"You will?" Wendy asked.
Gus nodded. "Uh-huh. I even drew a picture for you."
One of the armadillos nipped at Wendy's fingers.
She began to cry.
"How will I ever get to leave here and see it?" she asked.
Tears spilled down her cheeks.

Gus turned to Zub. "What can I give you to let her go?" He emptied his
pockets. He had five nickels, three pennies, and a stick of
cinnamon gum. He held them all out to Zub.
Zub brushed Gus's hands away.
"I need to feed my armadillos or else they won't do as I tell them.
If I let your sister go,
who's going to keep them fed with cupcakes?
I used to do the baking,
but it's much more fun watching your sister do it all.

"You and I have a deal," Zub went on.
"You made a trade because you were
a greedy, selfish boy
who wasn't thinking about his sister.
Well, now you have to live with your decision."

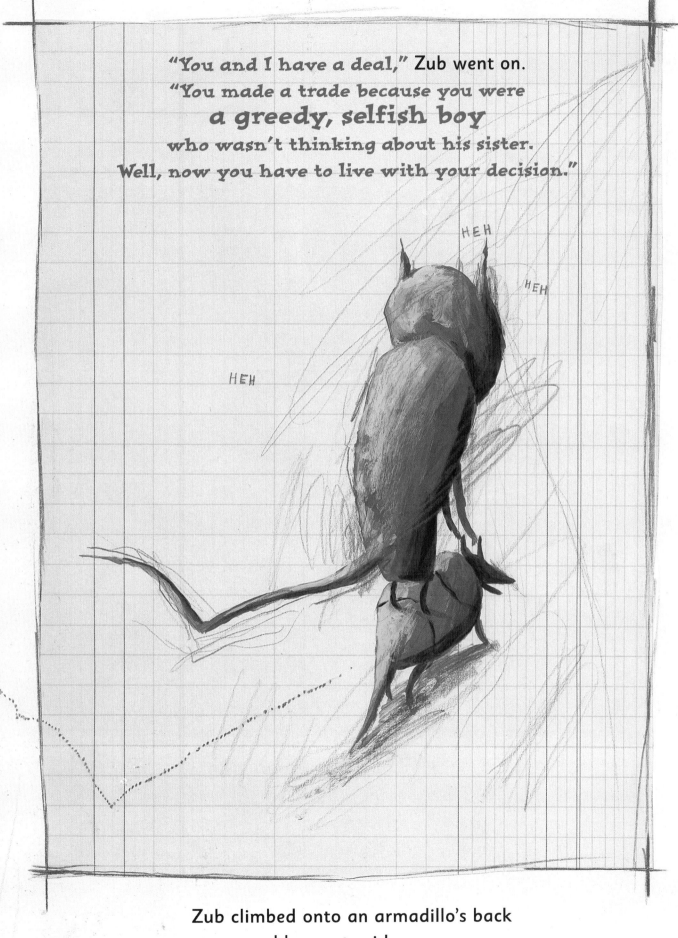

Zub climbed onto an armadillo's back
and began to ride away.

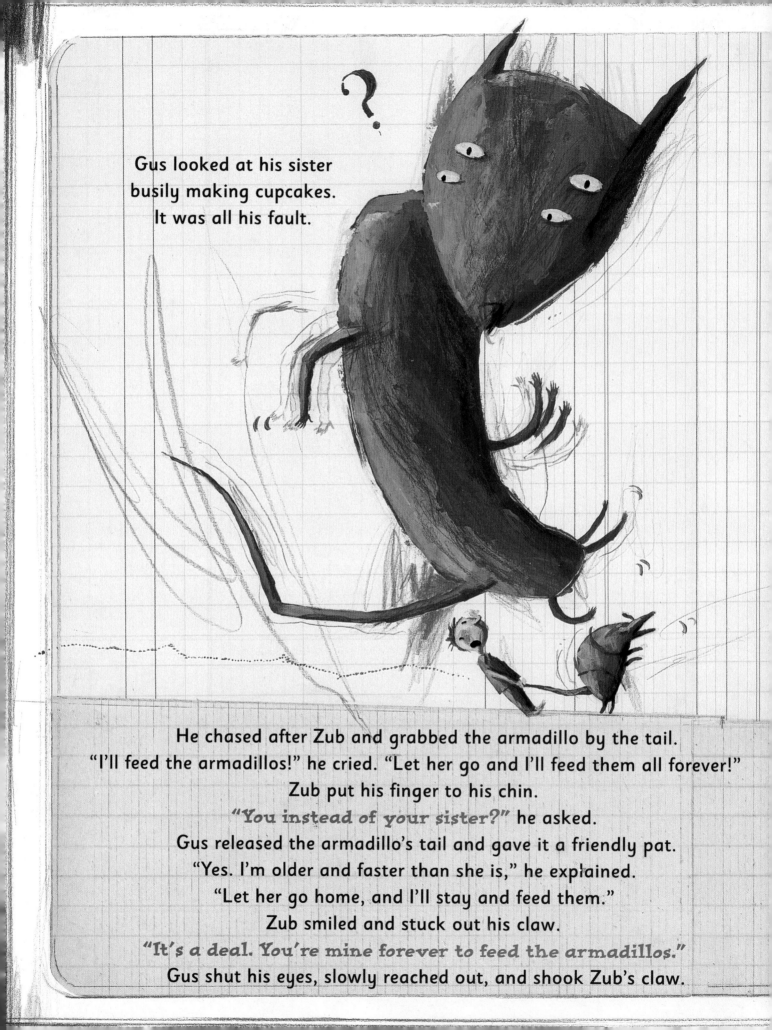

Gus looked at his sister
busily making cupcakes.
It was all his fault.

He chased after Zub and grabbed the armadillo by the tail.
"I'll feed the armadillos!" he cried. "Let her go and I'll feed them all forever!"
Zub put his finger to his chin.
"You instead of your sister?" he asked.
Gus released the armadillo's tail and gave it a friendly pat.
"Yes. I'm older and faster than she is," he explained.
"Let her go home, and I'll stay and feed them."
Zub smiled and stuck out his claw.
"It's a deal. You're mine forever to feed the armadillos."
Gus shut his eyes, slowly reached out, and shook Zub's claw.

There was a flash of lightning
and a clap of thunder.

When Gus opened his eyes,
he was face-to-face
with a long line of armadillos.

They snapped their jaws open and closed.
"**Hurry up and make those cupcakes,**"
Zub commanded.
"**My pets are hungry, hungry, hungry!**"
Gus glanced around. His sister was gone.
"Where's Wendy?" he asked.
Zub scratched an armadillo behind the ears.
"*She's back home. I always keep my end of a deal.* . . . .
**Now you keep yours and
feed my friends.**"

Gus reached for a cupcake to give to an armadillo.
Suddenly his feet lifted off the ground.
He began to float.

"No! No! No!"
Zub cried as he jumped to grab hold of Gus.
"Come down here!"
"What's happening?" Gus called. "Where am I going?"
He floated higher and higher, still holding the cupcake.
Zub frowned.
Gus was far too high for him to reach.
He waved a claw in the air.

"That must have been a sour deal
I made just now," he shouted.
"You traded for bad to get the crayons
and be rid of your sister.
But then you traded for good to send her home.
I should have known a trade for good wouldn't work."
Gus looked down.
The armadillos snapped at Zub's feet. They were hungry.
Zub hurried to mix more cupcake batter.

Gus soared higher. He was about to crash into a star
when he floated right through it and out of
the land of hungry armadillos.

Then he fell and fell and fell until—kerplunk—he landed on his bed. His sister was waiting for him.

"You're home!" Wendy shouted.

She jumped up and down and gave her big brother a hug.

Gus hugged her and smiled. "I am home," he said. "I really am sorry I traded you to Zub. I just wanted my own crayons and paper and to draw by myself."

Wendy nodded. "Sometimes I don't like having you around and want things all for myself too," she said.

"I forgive you." She looked at her brother. "Do you still really want your own crayons and paper?" she asked.

"Yeah." Gus grinned. "But not as much as I want you for a sister."

That afternoon,
Gus and Wendy sat in the living room.
They shared crayons and they shared paper.
Gus drew Wendy a picture of her on a pony.
Wendy drew Gus a picture of a dancing giraffe.
They fought only once,
when they both wanted
the Lima Bean Green crayon at the same time.
Gus gave it to his sister first,
and then he took a turn using it.
And for a snack,
Gus and Wendy shared the cupcake
Gus had brought all the way
from the land of hungry armadillos.

Wendy got half.
Gus got half.

And Zub and the hungry armadillos got none.